Kevin and the Triple Creature Feature

by

Martin Tiller

Illustrated by

Carla Tracy

ISBN-13: 978-0615995045 (Seven Lions Publishing)
ISBN-10: 0615995047

Dedication

Thanks to Jenny Call, Erin Ewing, Rita Fitch-Petit, Eleanor Green, Linda Johnson, Tracy Lopez, and Jay Lynn for reading and offering their support on this book.

Thanks to Carla for continuing to bring Kevin and his friends to life.

To my students, always be creative and make your own stories.

For Heather and Rachel

Table of Contents

Kevin and the Triple Creature Feature

Chapter 1 The Two Pirates

"Follow me! Land on the Falcon! She shall be ours! We shall avenge the White Whale!" Grey Beard, the pirate, pointed his sword forward, leading his crew towards the Falcon. The Falcon was the high-seas fastest ship, and it was going to be Grey Beard's.

Captain Kurtz leaned over the edge of the Falcon and spied Grey Beard through his spyglass. Captain Kurtz smiled and pulled out his sword. He turned to his crew, "Grey Beard is mine! Leave him alone! He is mine!"

Grey Beard's crew rowed to the side of the Falcon and began climbing the ship. They fought their way over the edge. Captain Kurtz took three steps back and waved Grey Beard towards himself.

"I've been waiting for you, Grey Beard!" He raised his sword and swung hard. Grey Beard blocked the swing and they began dueling on the deck of the Falcon.

"Your swing is weak, old man!" shouted Captain Kurtz.

"You can't win, Kurtz! The Falcon will be mine!" growled Grey Beard pushing Captain Kurtz backwards.

Chapter 2 It's Our Movie

"Hello! Kevin. Put the pencil down," said Jared Thompson. "It's time to go to school. The bus has stopped." Jared patted Kevin on the shoulder and walked around him. Kevin put down the pencil and got off the bus.

Kevin was busy writing a pirate story. The story had begun when he was daydreaming in class. His third grade teacher, Mrs. Calvin, instructed Kevin to record his daydreams. His pirate story was taking him several days to finish. It had been interrupted by Jared to make a movie, Attack of the Three-Headed Alien. Kevin wrote the story for the movie and starred in it. Now that it was over he was back to writing about Grey Beard and Captain Kurtz, two pirates of the seven seas.

Kevin and Jared walked into Mrs. Calvin's room. Jared hung up his backpack and pulled out a sheet of paper and handed it to Kevin. "Here is the flier."

Kevin looked at the flier. Jared had been working on a computer. A still picture from the movie, with the alien was centered in the middle of the flier. Attack of the Three-Headed Alien spread across the top in yellow. A screenshot of the alien was centered in the middle of the flier. The bottom had the details: "Movie screening - Saturday the 29th at Kevin Kershner's

4

House - 7 PM."

"This looks cool," said Kevin, looking at the flier.

"Mrs. Calvin, can we post this outside Mrs. Rivers' office?" said Jared. Mrs. Rivers was the guidance counselor, after all, and Jared thought she wouldn't mind. "What is it Jared?" asked Mrs. Calvin, who was standing at the classroom door, marking students present on the attendance sheet as they arrived.

"It's a flier for our movie that we made. I want to put some up here at school, like on the community bulletin board Mrs. Rivers has outside her office."

"Yes. You and Kevin can go and see if it is okay with her." Mrs. Calvin waved them out the door.

Outside Mrs. Rivers' office, Jared knocked on the slightly open door and Mrs. Rivers appeared. "Yes, Jared and Kevin?"

Jared handed her the flier. "Can we put this flier up on the community board? We want to show our movie to the neighborhood."

"Boys, that sounds like a wonderful idea!" Mrs. Rivers took the flier and looked it over. "Go ahead and post it on the board. I look forward to coming and seeing it."

Mrs. Rivers handed Jared a thumb tack, and he went into the hallway and put up the flier. "There we go!" Jared clapped his hands and smiled.

"What is that?" asked a boy with short, curly black hair.

"Oh, hey Mike. We're going to show our movie to the neighborhood. You want to come?" asked Kevin.

Mike Jefferies stood staring at the flier. "That sounds cool." He continued standing there. "How about I make a movie and bring it to show with your movie?"

Kevin and Jared stood still.

"But it's our movie," Jared finally said.

"Yeah, I know. But I want to make a movie too. Let's show them together."

Jared looked at Kevin. "But it's our movie," said Jared pointing between himself and Kevin.

"I know. I got to go class. I'll talk to you guys later." Mike walked away.

Jared turned and looked at Kevin, "But it's our movie!"

Chapter 3 Getting the Word Out

At lunch, Kevin and Jared sat together. "Where else do you think we should put up the flier?" asked Jared. Putting up a flier at school was not enough for him.

"I guess we can walk around the neighborhood and put up fliers, like people do for yard sales and lost cats."

"I agree," said Sarah Rose as she sat down with the boys. She also starred in the movie. "I think we could begin putting fliers up this afternoon."

"I'd have to ask my parents first," replied Kevin. "I don't think walking around the neighborhood by ourselves would fly with them."

"My dad said he would be willing to help with whatever was needed," said Sam Ford. His role in the movie was ordering a bombing attack on the alien, with the now-famous line, "Send in the bombers!"

"He could go with us around the neighborhood if your parents can't go," continued Sam.

"Okay, so we'll put fliers up around the neighborhood. Any other ideas on how to let people know about the movie?" asked Jared.

"I'll let my cub scout troop know," said TJ Williams, who had the starring role as the alien.

"Sweet," said Jared.

"Give me a flier as well, and I will give it to my dance teacher. Maybe she'll put it up at her dance studio," said Sarah, sipping on her milk.

"Thanks everyone. It sounds like we have a lot of good places to tell about the movie. I'll call you tonight Sam and let you know if I can go with you around the neighborhood," said Kevin. "This sounds like it just might work."

Jared rubbed his hands together and laughed a sinister laugh, "Yes! It is going to work! It is going to work! Yes, my precious!"

The whole table laughed.

Chapter 4 Double Feature

Later at recess, after running a lap around the track, Jared caught up with Kevin. "Let's go shoot basketball."

"Sure," Kevin replied. Kevin went over to the ball bag and pulled out a basketball.

Mike Jefferies ran over. "Hey guys, Jordan and Jason want to make a movie too and show it with your movie."

Jared and Kevin looked at each other. "It's our movie, our show," said Jared, pointing at Kevin and himself.

"Why can't we make a movie and show it with you guys?" Mike shrugged his shoulders.

"That's not what my mom is prepared for. Plus, the fliers we made only mention our movie," Kevin replied.

"Good point!" Jared said, agreeing with Kevin.

"You could make our movie like a bonus. We would be the surprise in a double feature."

Kevin looked at Mike, "I need to ask my parents. Another movie would bring more people."

"We should totally do this. It would be very cool," Mike said, as he jogged away to go throw a football with other classmates.

Kevin started dribbling the basketball. "The idea of another movie may help bring more people to see our movie," said Kevin as he shot the ball into the hoop.

Jared took the rebound and shot the ball, "Yeah, but we worked hard on our movie. I want to show it off. I don't want to share with someone else."

"Imagine if someone told you to not make Attack of the Three-Headed Alien. What would you do?" Kevin asked.

Jared smiled and took a deep breath, "I would work even harder to make the movie." Jared took the ball and made a lay-up.

Mrs. Calvin blew the whistle for the class to line up. Kevin and Jared took the basketball and got in line.

Kevin began walking with his class when he felt a tap on his shoulder. He turned around and saw Alex Hamner. Another third grader, but he was in Mrs. Wilson's class. "Hey, Manuel and I want in. We want to make a movie and show it with yours. We're thinking a superhero movie. That cool with you?"

Kevin just looked at Alex and said "Ummm." But Kevin's class moved on before he could really respond to Alex.

As they walked into the school Jared and Kevin looked at each other. What had they created?

Chapter 5 The Treasure of Lima

Captain Kurtz fell backwards and hit the deck of the Falcon. Grey Beard pointed his sword down at Kurtz, "Yield the Falcon to me!"

"Never!" Kurtz swung his sword and pushed away Grey Beard's sword. Kurtz jumped to his feet. He swung his sword, making Grey Beard jump backwards.

Kurtz looked at Grey Beard, "You have no idea of the treasure which we are looking for! One beyond your imagination. More wealth than you can possibly imagine!"

"I don't know. I can imagine quite a bit!" Grey Beard swung his sword.

Kurtz leapt backwards, "I know where the Treasure of Lima is!"

Grey Beard's sword froze in midair.

The Treasure of Lima was the most famous treasure of all. The most expensive, the most impressive.

Kurtz held out his hand, "Together we can find the treasure of Lima! Without me you'll never see it!"

Grey Beard dropped his sword to his side.

"Kevin! Get up! Your bus stop!" shouted Jared.

Startled, Kevin stood up, closed his journal, placed his pencil in his pocket and rushed off the bus. Jared followed closely behind.

"Hey! Wait a minute!" said Jared. "What are you working on? You're on to something, aren't you?"

Kevin walked briskly as he slid his backpack on, "What are you talking about?" said Kevin hoping that Jared would leave him alone.

"You got distracted again, I know you were adding to the pirate story. The story sucked you in. Let me read it," said Jared, sticking his hand out to Kevin.

Kevin stopped. He learned to not fight Jared when he began asking questions like this. "Ugh! Okay, follow me home. I'll show you what I got." Exasperated, Kevin briskly walked to his house. Jared followed closely behind.

The boys walked in the front door, and up the stairs to Kevin's room. They dropped their backpacks in the corner, and Kevin handed his journal to Jared. Jared collapsed on the bed and began reading.

Jared was quiet as he flipped through the story. Kevin sat in a chair and stared at the ceiling. He knew to not interrupt Jared.

"The Treasure of Lima? I like it," said Jared. "It's like Indiana Jones meets pirates. And that's a couple of levels of awesome."

Jared closed the journal, laid down on the bed and stared at the ceiling.

Jared asked, "How can they all of a sudden get along if they have been fighting?"

Kevin replied, "Well, they are pirates. Finding treasure is what they do. The Treasure of Lima is a legendary treasure. Sort of the treasure all pirates are looking for. That is something most pirates can work together for."

"So where do they go? How does Kurtz keep the treasure a secret? What happens when they do find the treasure? What does Grey Beard do with Kurtz then?" Jared rattled off question after question.

"I have my ideas."

"And?" Jared leaned forward.

"You'll just have to read the story when it's finished."

Jared smiled and fell back down on Kevin's bed.

Kevin grabbed the journal off the bed and sat down at his desk. Jared stayed still. Apparently, he wasn't leaving. Kevin put the journal on his desk and started writing. He ignored Jared. Jared had just sort of inserted himself into Kevin's life.

"Let's make the pirate movie," said Jared.

Kevin kept writing. "What pirate movie?"

"The story you are working on now. The Treasure of Lima. Let's make that movie!" Jared sat up.

Kevin put down his pencil and looked at Jared, "We already have a movie to show. What are you talking about?"

"Yes. And now we can have two," said Jared.

"No. We're too busy getting ready for the film festival, which was way more than I was expecting in the first place," said Kevin, not looking up, still writing.

Jared stared at the ceiling and remained quiet.

A smile appeared on Jared's face. He jumped off the bed and bounded out the door. "It's a cool story, buddy. I will catch you later!" Jared ran down the stairs and shot out the front door. Kevin shrugged his shoulders and went back to writing about pirates.

Chapter 6 They'll Come

"Mr. Ford is coming over after supper to help us pass out fliers for the movie," said Mrs. Kershner, Kevin's mother.

Mr. Ford was Sam's dad. Sam played an army officer that yelled into a green phone, "Send in the bombers!" Sam loved that line so much he began saying it at school. The others students found it funny when Sam would answer a teacher's question with "Send in the bombers!" It was funny when a question about Christopher Columbus was answered with "Send in the bombers!" Mrs. Calvin wasn't amused.

Kevin's was mom was spooning mashed potatoes onto his plate. "So where do you think we should post the fliers?"

Kevin took his plate. "Well, definitely up and down our street, the library, and outside the church on the corner of Maple."

"Smart idea- those areas get a lot of foot traffic during the week," said Kevin's dad as he shoveled potatoes and gravy into his mouth.

"POTATOES!" shouted Michael, Kevin's little brother.

"Don't shout at the dinner table, Michael," his mom

said calmly. The doorbell rang.

"That must be Mr. Ford." Kevin's mom wiped her mouth with her napkin. "Don't forget to say thank you."

Kevin rolled his eyes as he scooted his chair back and got down from the table.

Kevin opened the door and there stood Mr. Ford and his son. "Sam! Cool! I didn't realize you were coming."

"Of course he is going to come and help- he is in the movie," Mr. Ford smirked and nudged Sam on the back.

"Send in the bombers!" said Sam, smiling.

Kevin's dad came walking to the door with Michael. "Nice to see you guys again." He shook Mr. Ford's hand.

"I'll meet you guys outside in a minute," Mrs. Kershner said from the kitchen. Kevin's dad grabbed Michael's stroller and they headed outside.

"I have the fliers," said Kevin. "I brought a stapler." Mr. Ford raised his hand with the stapler.

The front door shut and Mrs. Kershner walked out and clapped her hands. "Okay! Let's go spread the word!"

For the next thirty minutes they walked up and down the street, stapling fliers to telephone poles. They got to the end of the neighborhood and turned onto Maple Street, where a lot of people walked and a lot of cars drove past.

Sam raised his hand with a stack of fliers, "I have about ten fliers left. We can put several fliers on the telephone poles on each corner."

After they finished, Kevin and Sam looked at their work. The fliers were noticeable from all four corners of the intersection. Kevin and Sam looked at each other and celebrated with a fist bump.

"Here's to hoping people will come. We need to think of another way to get the word out," said Kevin.

"Trust me. They'll come," said Sam quietly.

Chapter 7 500 Students

The next day at school, Kevin sat down at lunch with the crew- Jared, Sarah, Sam and TJ.

"I saw the fliers this morning from the school bus. Great job," said Sarah as she opened her milk.

"What are some other ways that we can let people know about the festival?" asked Kevin.

Sarah put her milk down, "You put up a flier outside of Mrs. River's office and most people here at school know. That's about 500 students. Exactly how many people need to know about this?"

Kevin's stomach sank. She was right. How can his parents potentially host 100 or so people? Forget his parents- 100 people at his house? What if they want to see his room? What if they make fun of his house or the stuff he has in his room?

"Wait until you see our movie!" Mike Jefferies stood over the table. "My dad just got a new camera, and we have a dragon in ours. It's going to be sweet!"

"So?" Sam shrugged his shoulders.

"Didn't Kevin say we could show a movie with your movie?" said Mike.

The table looked at Kevin.

"No, I didn't. It's OUR movie," Kevin gestured around the whole table.

"Oh, come on! It would be fun. It would bring more people to see your movie," said Mike, trying to convince the table.

Sarah put her fork down, and looked at Kevin.

Mike waved his arm, "Okay, fine. We'll do our own festival, and I'll get Alex to bring his movie with us. We'll be making a dragon movie, and they'll be making a super hero movie. I wonder which movie showing will get more people?" and he walked away.

Sarah furrowed her brow, "You know. He may be right. We let them join, then they bring people to see their movies, which then brings people to see our movie. Because in spite of putting up all the fliers, there is no telling just how many people will come to see us. But at least this way we know that our friends and their friends will come see it."

The crew was quiet.

TJ put down his milk, "She has a point- more people to see us."

Kevin's heart began to pound through his chest. Now there would be two more movies at his house?

"We could show their movies first and then show ours. We would get top billing." Jared's producing skills were coming out.

"And we could have a vote on which movie was better," said Sarah, and she smiled as she said it.

"And we could give out other awards, such as best actor or actress, or best special effects," said Sam.

"I like these ideas. Yeah, let's do it!" Jared grinned ear to ear.

"Wait! My parents are preparing for just our movie." Kevin spoke firmly.

"But they helped pass out all those fliers, so they are expecting some people to come," said Sarah.

TJ spoke up, "And it's not like your parents have to do it all by themselves. Most of our parents helped with making the movie."

"Yeah, remember my dad came by and helped pass out fliers," Sam reminded Kevin.

"This will work Kevin, and it's going to be a blast! Stop worrying so much!" Jared patted Kevin on the back.

Mrs. Calvin called for the class to line up.

Kevin got into line without saying a thing. How did he get himself into this? What were his parents going to say?

Kevin didn't say a thing the rest of the school day.

Chapter 8 The Triple Feature

Kevin was quiet at the dinner table.

"Kevin, pass the green beans please," said Mrs. Kershner.

Kevin stared off into space. He was terrified to tell his parents. Two more movies?

"Kevin!" his dad raised his voice. Kevin woke up, looked around, and handed the plate of green beans to his mother.

His mother had had enough, "Okay, what is going on? You haven't said anything since you got home from school."

No point in waiting, "Jared wants to have two other groups over to show their movies," Kevin paused, waiting for the yelling to begin. "I can tell them to call it off."

His mom looked at his dad, and then she turned and looked at him. "Kevin, that seems like a wonderful idea!"

Kevin stopped chewing his food.

"After all, you told Mrs. Rivers at school, and you put

all of those fliers up around the neighborhood. Why not share in the fun?" His mother shrugged off the worry.

"Who are the other groups? Anybody we know?" Asked his dad.

"Mike Jefferies wants to make a movie, and so does Alex Hamner."

Mr. Kershner asked "Mike is in your class right? Who is Alex?"

"Alex is in Mrs. Wilson's class," replied Kevin.

"Well, I am fine with it. We'll need their parents' phone numbers and emails," said his mother.

Great, more work to do, thought Kevin. How did I get stuck with this? Kevin drank his water.

"That would make three movies. You could call it a Triple Creature Feature!" His dad was smiling at the thought. "Before cable TV, DVDs and video games, children would go to the movies on Saturday and watch monster or science fiction movies, and often there were two or more movies together. Two movies together would be called a double feature and three together would be called a triple feature. You could sell this as a triple feature, and since at least your movie has a creature in it, you name it the Triple Creature Feature." His dad was grinning ear to ear. He was quite happy with his idea.

"Okay, can I be dismissed? I need to call Jared and let him know," asked Kevin.

"Yes, take your dishes to the sink please," said his mother.

Kevin went to the living room, picked up the phone and called Jared. He told Jared the news- the other movies were allowed in.

Kevin could hear Jared smiling on the other end of the phone.

Chapter 9 Competition

The next morning Kevin and Jared walked into Mrs. Calvin's room and hung up their backpacks. Mike came in behind them.

"My cousin Molly is going to be our movie. She's done some professional acting." Mike quite clearly was showing off a little.

"What has she been in?" Jared asked.

"She's been in commercials."

"Which ones? Anything we've seen?" Jared shrugged his shoulders.

"You probably haven't seen them," Mike continued.

"Okay, whatever," and with that Jared waved his hand and walked away from Mike.

"What is your movie about?" Kevin asked, trying to be polite.

"It has a dragon, a princess, and a knight. And the princess does the rescuing," said Mike.

"Have you made it yet?"

"No, we're shooting this weekend at my house. It will be awesome!" Mike made a fist and pumped it in the air.

The bell rang and all the students went to their seats to begin their morning work.

Later, during lunch, Kevin sat down with the rest of the crew- Jared, Sarah, TJ, and Sam.

"Mike told me that they are making a movie with a dragon," announced Kevin.

"That sounds cool," replied TJ.

"But what if people like their movie more than ours?" wondered Kevin.

"Our movie is awesome. Don't worry about it," said Sam squirting ketchup onto a pile of French fries.

"Is this supposed to be a competition anyway?" asked Sam.

"We could have a vote! We could vote for the best actor, and best actress, best director, and best writer," said Sarah, pointing to Kevin.

Jared was quiet, he was thinking. "How would that work? Wouldn't those people that come to see us vote for us, and those that come for the other movies, vote for those movies? Wouldn't that take the fun out of this? If people like our movie won't they just tell us?"

"That's a good point, plus everyone will know which movie is best anyway without having to vote," TJ smiled.

"Hey!" Shouted Manuel Johnson from another table. The crew turned around.

"Ours will be the best. Ours has superheroes in it." Manuel was smiling.

"What movie?" asked Jared.

"Mine and Alex's movie. Ours has superheroes! We win," Manuel pointed to himself.

The crew turned around, ignoring Manuel. "Ugh! When did this become a competition?" Kevin said to no one in particular.

Jared smiled. "Yes. This will be a competition."

The crew looked at him. "What do you mean?" said Sarah.

"It will be a competition to see who can get more people to come to the festival." Jared was grinning ear to ear.

Sam smiled, and then it turned to an evil grin. "Yes. Let's this be a competition. Yes. Let it be." Sam began to cackle.

"You okay?" asked TJ.

Sam continued to grin. "Yes. Let the competition begin."

He put his hands down on the table and spoke quietly, "Send in the bombers! Send in the bombers!" The rest of the crew turned and looked at each other. Sam had lost his mind.

Luckily, Mrs. Calvin called for the class to line up before Sam lost his mind even more.

Chapter 10 Multiplication War

Kevin sat down at his desk and pulled out his math journal. After finishing the word problem on the board, he moved to sit down with Jared. Jared had a packet of playing cards. The boys practiced their multiplication facts by pulling two cards, multiplying them, and then the partner with the greatest number would keep the cards. Mrs. Calvin called it "Multiplication Collection," but the boys in class called it "Multiplication War." Mrs. Calvin didn't like that title.

Kevin pulled out a 9 and a 6. "54," said Kevin.

Jared put down a 7 and a 3. "21" said Jared.

"I win," said Kevin, and he took two his cards and put them to the side.

"You know we will have a professional actress in our movie," whispered Alex from the table nearby.

Jared and Kevin looked over at Alex, and Jared rolled his eyes. "So what?" Jared shrugged his shoulders.

Alex leaned over to them and continued to whisper, "You know people will like our movie better!"

"Go away," whispered Kevin.

"Kevin!" spoke Mrs. Calvin firmly from across the room.

"Alex is bothering us, Mrs. Calvin," Kevin explained.

Alex quickly went back to working on his multiplication problems. "I am just working here," pleaded Alex.

Jared came to Kevin's rescue, "No, Mrs. Calvin, Alex is bothering us."

"Enough boys. Alex stay on your work with your table." Mrs. Calvin rolled her eyes and went back to working with students at her table.

Alex hid a smile.

Jared threw down a 7 and an 8. "56!" he shouted.

Kevin drew a 9 and a 3, "27."

"I win!" exclaimed Jared.

"You won't at the film festival in a couple of weeks," whispered Alex.

"Oh please, your cousin was in a stupid car commercial. It wasn't like she was in a Broadway play!" responded Jared.

"Yeah, well it's more than you guys have got," Alex got louder.

"You haven't even seen our movie, you don't know what you are talking about," said Kevin, and he got louder as he spoke.

"Okay boys! Back to your seats. What is going on between you three?" Mrs. Calvin stood up and walked toward the boys.

Kevin and Jared stayed at the table with their playing cards. "I told you two to go back to your seats."

Jared pleaded, "We didn't do anything, Mrs. Calvin! Alex keeps messing with us."

"Come see me, Kevin and Jared," said Mrs. Calvin.

The boys looked at each other, rolled their eyes, stood up, and walked over to Mrs. Calvin's desk.

Jared went first, "Alex won't let us work. He keeps leaning over and telling us that he is going to win at our film festival."

Mrs. Calvin nodded. "I have heard about your film festival. It sounds like fun."

"You've heard about it?" Kevin's eyes got bigger.

"Kevin, you guys did put a flier outside of Mrs. Rivers. I do work here," she explained.

Kevin felt a little silly.

"But I cannot have you guys interrupting class anymore. You have work to do, and the other students have work to do as well."

"We know! We've been trying to work. Alex won't leave us alone!" Jared couldn't stand it anymore.

"Jared, enough!" Mrs. Calvin furrowed her brow. "Your parents will need to know about your interrupting class today. You'll both have notes that will need to be signed and brought back."

Kevin's stomach sank. He knew today was going to be the last day he would ever live. This is what a condemned man must feel like.

"Mrs. Calvin!" Jared raised his voice.

"Jared! Don't make it worse. Just come work over here by me." She pointed to a couple of open desks near her.

The boys sat down and continued to work. This time without saying a word. Kevin heard Alex chuckle a few feet away, and Kevin's face turned red.

Seeing the note later in the day nearly made Kevin cry. He knew there would be no more film festival after this. Interrupting school was a big deal with his parents. So first, there would be no more film festival. And then they would kill him.

They would kill him.

Chapter 11 Your Teacher Called

Kevin got off the bus. He didn't hear Jared say, "It will be all right." He walked in the door and there was his mother feeding his little brother Michael, who was too young to go to school.

"How was school?" His mom asked.

He mumbled, "Fine." And he ran upstairs to his room and shut the door. Kevin flung himself onto the bed. And buried his face into the pillows. He just laid there.

There was a knock on the door. "Kevin?" It was his mom.

"Yes?"

"Can I come in?"

"Umm…yes." Kevin replied.

His mom slowly opened the door and peered her head in.

"Kevin, Mrs. Calvin called me this afternoon after school."

Kevin froze in fear.

"Do you want to talk about it?" his mother asked.

"What did she say? What did she want to talk about?" Kevin had learned to not assume that he parents knew everything.

"Well, she said there is a note in your backpack that I need to sign. That you and Jared were being disruptive during math today."

In this case, his parents did know what was going on.

Kevin rolled off of his bed, unzipped his backpack, and handed the note to his mom. She opened it and read it silently.

After what seemed to be a million years, she put the note down, signed it, and handed it back to Kevin.

"So what is your side of the story?" she asked.

"Alex was bothering us. He was teasing us. Saying that his movie is going to be better than ours at the film festival."

"Well, I am sorry that happened. I didn't realize it was going to be a competition."

"I didn't realize it either," replied Kevin.

"Next time he bothers you in class, ask to see if you can move to somewhere else in the room, as opposed to disrupting the class. You may have been known for falling asleep in class or daydreaming, but it is nice to know that you don't have a reputation for disrupting class. Your father and I would like to keep it that way. And knowing Jared, my guess is that he helped make the situation worse. So maybe you need to walk away from Jared as well, if this happens again."

Kevin sat listening, and imagining trying to walk away from Jared and telling him to stop. He had tried that before. It didn't work.

He laughed to himself thinking about stopping Jared.

"What's so funny?" Mrs. Kershner asked.

Kevin shook his head, "Nothing."

"Well, no more notes like this from school. We won't talk about this anymore, even when dad gets home. Just don't let this happen again." And she walked out of Kevin's room.

Kevin grabbed his journal, and rolled back onto his bed, and began writing about pirates.

Chapter 12 Pirates Are Cool

The next day was Friday. The film festival was two Saturdays away. During recess Kevin and Jared were shooting basketball.

"You still don't want to make another movie?" asked Jared, as he took a shot from the foul line. The ball made a swooshing sound as it went through the basket.

"Not now I don't. We have too much to do for next weekend. What would we make anyway?" said Kevin has he took a shot.

"You know the pirate movie."

"I'm beginning to wish you had never seen that story," replied Kevin. His shot missed completely. John Levon, a boy in another class, threw the ball back as he walked by.

Jared grabbed the ball, "Thanks." Jared waved his hand at John. Jared turned around and passed the ball back to Kevin as hard as he could.

"The movie will be good." Jared said as he threw the ball back

"We already have a good movie." Kevin took the ball,

and made a lay-up this time.

Jared continued, "But its fun to make a movie. Admit it. It was fun. All those other guys are going to be making their movies this weekend. They're going to be creative this weekend. Look, the pirate story is just very good. You need to do something with that story."

"Thanks, I admit I like it too. Maybe next Halloween we can dress up as pirates."

"You have another movie to make?" asked Sam, who was standing near the basketball court. He and TJ were looking for something to do when they saw Kevin and Jared talking.

Kevin got exasperated, "No! I do not have another movie to make."

"He is working on a pirate story that is pretty cool," explained Jared.

"Pirates are cool," said TJ.

"Show us the story," demanded Sam.

"I don't have my journal outside with me," said Kevin, spreading his arms out as if he was looking for the missing journal.

"Well, when can we see it?" asked Sam.

Kevin paused and then looked at Jared. "You really gotta stop this. No more telling people about the stuff I am working on."

Jared furrowed his brow and shrugged his shoulders, "Why are you mad at me? It's a good story, just like the alien one. Share it with people. You are good at this."

Sam looked at Jared, "Do you think we have enough time to make this movie before the festival?"

"No," said Kevin. "We would have to make pirate costumes and make a pirate set. Remember the reason the last movie worked was because we were able to use my backyard as the set. We don't have anything that looks remotely like a pirate ship to work with."

Sam and TJ looked at each other and nodded. "Leave the costumes and the set to us."

Kevin stood there with the basketball on his hip and his mouth wide open. "The other problem is that I haven't finished writing the story yet."

Sam shrugged his shoulders, "So! You're good. You'll finish it soon."

Kevin just put his hands in the air as if to surrender.

Then the bell rang, and Kevin hoped that would end this nonsense.

Chapter 13 Visiting the Set

The next Saturday morning at 10 am Kevin was watching anime cartoons and eating a bowl of Cheerios, when the doorbell rang.

"Kevin, see who it is," his dad told him from the basement.

Kevin went to the door, turned the knob and began opening the door when Jared pushed through. He was in a hurry.

"Man, you got to see this." Jared looked Kevin up and down. "Get dressed. We are going to go check out Alex and their movie. They are working on it right now."

"Where are they?"

"Right down the street over at Alex's house. I saw them filming when I was walking the dog this morning."

Kevin looked at his pajamas, ran into the kitchen, threw his bowl into the sink, and ran upstairs. Jared followed him.

They ran into Kevin's room. "What did you see?" said Kevin frantically as he began pulling clothes out of a drawer.

"I saw a guy dressed up in tights. Blue tights with a cape. Then I saw an adult dressed in some dark outfit. Looked like he might be some sort of villain."

"A grown-up? They're using grownups?" Kevin's voice became louder as he spoke. Having the movie be all kids from the school just seemed to be an unwritten rule.

At least Kevin thought it was an unwritten rule. After all their movie was made with all third graders. No adults needed.

Fully dressed Kevin rushed out of his room and down the stairs. "Mom, Jared and I are going down the street to Alex's house."

"Okay. Wait which house is that?" Mrs. Kershner replied.

Kevin and Jared ran out the door and then shouted behind him, "The one with the superheroes out in the front yard."

Kevin and Jared ran down the street. They passed four houses and ran up a hill. As they reached the top of the hill Kevin saw what Jared was talking about. There was a six foot man dressed in a black outfit. It looked like a modified Batman costume. Kevin and Jared froze, and just watched the scene unfold in front of them.

Their classmate, Alex, was standing there in a bright blue outfit shouting at the villain. Another student was standing behind a camera that was set on a tripod. Some other actors were standing behind the camera dressed as superheroes in bright, colorful costumes.

As the scene continued Alex's voice grew louder and louder and his right hand was pointing more and more firmly at the villainous adult. Suddenly Alex yelled "cut!" waved his hand and everyone began milling around the camera to take a look at what had just been shot.

"What do you think?" Jared asked Kevin.

Kevin replied, "I admit, from what I see here, it looks pretty interesting."

"Hey Kevin! Jared!" Alex was waving at them. "You guys come to see what a great movie we are making?" In spite of the mask he was wearing, Alex was quite clearly grinning from ear to ear.

The villainous adult put his hand on Alex's back and whispered in his ear. Alex nodded. The villainous adult began jogging toward Kevin and Jared.

Kevin and Jared stood still.

The adult villain stuck out his hand, "Hi, Kevin. I'm Mr. Hamner. Alex's dad."

Kevin shook his hand.

"I am very impressed that you have put this little film festival together. I can't wait to see Attack of the Three-Headed Alien. I bet we could learn a lot from you guys on how to make a movie."

Kevin and Jared weren't sure what to say. They would have never expected Alex's dad to be this nice.

"Umm, thank you Mr. Hamner. I can't wait to see your movie. You must be playing a villain," replied Kevin.

"Yes. Call me Dr. Versa." Mr. Hamner put out his chest and his hands on his hips. He grinned. "Anyway, it was nice to meet you. I need to get back to the set!" Mr. Hamner chuckled at that comment. "You guys are more than welcome to stay and watch."

"We don't want to spoil the movie," said Jared.

"Of course!" Mr. Hamner ran back to his yard where children dressed in superhero costumes were waiting for him.

Kevin and Jared stayed where they were watching the filming.

"Jared! Kevin!" They turned around to see Sam, TJ, and Sarah walking toward them. "I just passed Mike's house. You gotta come see what they are doing." Sam paused and then pointed to the superheroes. "Wait is that Alex's movie being made down there?"

"Yup," replied Jared.

"And is that his dad in a superhero costume?"

"He's a villain," said Kevin.

"Is that fair? Using an adult?" Sam was frustrated.

"We never set ground rules," Kevin replied.

"But still!" complained Sam.

"His dad is dressed in a Halloween outfit, and is going to be seen by just about everyone in school. Do you think he will be cool after that?" said Jared.

Sam thought for a minute, "Good point."

Kevin was ready to go. "I've seen enough. Let's go see what Mike is doing."

Since this was a matter of urgency, they turned around and began running toward Mike's house. They ran past Kevin's house, and took a right and then a left. They stopped to catch their breath, and began walking towards Mike's house.

It was easy to find his house. There on the front lawn was a huge dragon. A dragon that seemed to have six feet.

"Look! They have three people in that dragon!" Sam said, pointing and shouting.

The dragon seemed to be made of some fabric. The front with the face must have been made of cardboard. There were two eyes painted on each side of the dragon. The mouth held about ten very sharp teeth. They looked like they were made from plastic mayonnaise jars. Scales were painted onto the sides.

"Their dragon has arms," Jared observed, and there was a sense of awe in his voice.

The person in the front of the dragon put their arms through sleeves and waved them around. The head of the dragon fit over the head of the person in front. The other two people were underneath a large piece of fabric. Green and gray scales were painted all over the body of the dragon. The fabric went low enough to the ground that it covered the legs of the two people in the body and tail section.

"Action!" yelled a girl behind the camera. The dragon came to life, and its front arms reached for the sky. The body of the dragon stooped close to the ground. A loud scream came from the dragon.

"Man, I really hope they add to that scream in post-production," said Sam.

Another blood-curdling scream arose, but the boys could not see where it was coming from. From the side of the house came running a knight, complete with a large sword.

"I wonder if my mom would make me one of those," asked TJ to himself.

"I'll make you one, it's simply cardboard and foil," said Sam.

"So what? Let's see you make one that looks like that. That sword looks awesome," replied TJ.

The knight swung the sword over his head and then made a slashing motion at the dragon. The dragon grabbed its chest and collapsed.

The camera kept rolling, so no one spoke.

The knight pulled off his helmet. When he did, the crew realized that the knight wasn't a he, but a she. She flipped her curly brown hair as she pulled the helmet off.

"So, she got the lead," said Sarah. "That must be the cousin who is a 'professional' actress." Sarah used air quotes around the word professional.

Kevin felt bad, "Don't worry, she might not be any good. Everyone knows you're a good actress."

"And cut!" yelled the girl behind the camera.

The actors in the dragon began taking off their costume. Mike Jefferies was the head of the dragon, and two other boys from class, Jason Smith and Hollis Coleman, were the body and tail of the dragon.

Mike turned around and saw the crew standing on the sidewalk. He waved. "Hey guys! Come on down and see the dragon!"

The crew looked at each other. "We should go and be polite," Kevin said.

"And cool. We should be cool," continued Sam.

The crew walked down the street, with Kevin in front.

"Your dragon looks cool." Kevin pointed at the dragon costume.

"Thanks, we worked on it all week."

The girl in the knight's outfit came walking up and put her hand out to Kevin.

"Hi, I'm Molly."

"I'm Kevin." Kevin had never had a girl his age ask to shake his hand before.

"Yes. I know. I've heard about you," said Molly. Kevin blushed. "Thank you for doing this film festival. It's pretty impressive what you have done."

"Well, it's all just supposed to be fun." Kevin was uncomfortable with all of the attention.

"Hi, I'm Molly." She put her hand out to Sarah. Kevin and Jared looked at them.

Sarah smiled, "Hi, I'm Sarah. I can't wait to see you in your movie." For a moment no one said a word.

Molly smiled, "I can't wait to see Attack of the Three-Headed Alien. I bet you're great!"

Sarah relaxed and smiled more. "Thank you," she said.

"Well, we'll let you get back to making your movie. You guys working on it all day?" Asked Kevin.

Mike replied, "Yup. We are following what you guys did. Shoot during the day, and edit in the evening."

"Well, we're going to go. Good luck. It looks great!" Kevin turned around and lead the crew away from the movie set and back to his house.

Chapter 14 Let's Go Write a Movie

The crew walked back into Kevin's room.

Sarah went first, "They look like good movies."

"Yeah, they might actually be better than ours," said Sam. The room became quiet.

"Look, so what if the other movies look good. Does that take away from the movie we made? After all, they're making movies because we made movies. Isn't that a good thing?" Kevin looked around the room.

Sam piped up, "Our movie is awesome."

Jared looked around the room, "Kevin has another story we can make a movie with."

Kevin rolled his eyes. "Okay, enough Jared. We can make the movie later."

"Well, read us the story," Sarah said.

"Can you read us this story that Jared is talking about? What's the story?" Asked TJ.

Kevin pulled his journal off his desk and thumbed to the pirate story.

"Okay, this is a pirate story." Kevin began reading about Captain Kurtz and the Treasure of Lima.

Kevin sat on the edge of bed and read aloud. His friends sat quietly around his room, listening to the story.

He reached the end of the story, where Captain Kurtz and Grey Beard made a pact to go in search of the Treasure of Lima together. Kevin closed his journal.

"And that's as far as I have gotten."

"My mom has pirate stuff we can use," said TJ.

"We can use the wooden swing set in my backyard to make the pirate ship," added Sam.

"I have a tree house in my yard that we could use as the bird's nest of the ship," Sarah said.

"What does a bird's nest have to do with anything?" Asked Sam.

"A bird's nest is the place where people sit at the top to look around at the ocean from high up," explained Sarah.

"Oh."

"I want to wait until after the festival. I am too worried about having everyone over here next weekend. We can make the movie after that. Does that work for everyone?" Kevin looked around the room.

Jared spoke up, "I told Mrs. Calvin about your pirate story."

"She knows I write stories. It was her that told me to begin writing, remember?"

"She told me that she would like you to put the story in the school newspaper," Jared explained.

"Why did you do that?" Kevin was angry.

The room got quiet.

"Because it is a good story," said Jared.

Kevin took a deep breath.

"Thanks, I guess. I'll think about it." Kevin waffled a little. "Maybe I'll finish it this week."

Sarah spoke up, "I have an idea. Let's go outside and act out this story. Maybe we help Kevin and help write the ending of the story together. Everyone cool with that?"

The friends looked at each other and nodded.

"I'll never turn down playing pirates," said Sam.

"Yeah, that sounds like fun." Said TJ standing up.

Jared jumped up smiling ear to ear, "Yes! Let's go write a movie!"

The crew went outside. For the rest of the day they ran around acting out pirate scenes and having fun.

Chapter 15 Getting Ready

The next week at school went by very slowly for Kevin and the rest of the crew. They all had an extra hard time staying focused in class. All they could think about was the premiere of their movie to people outside of their families. What was that going to be like?

Mercifully, Friday came, and the bell rang for the end of the school day. As Kevin was picking up his backpack to go home, Sam came and patted him on the back. "My dad and I will be over this afternoon to help set everything up." Sam grinned. "I can't wait!"

As Kevin got off the bus he saw that there were already several folding chairs out in his backyard. Kids on the bus noticed as well.

"Ooooh!" several of the kids said pointing to the chairs as Kevin and Jared were getting off the bus.

Jared followed Kevin to his house. "I am going to come help!" Grinned Jared.

Jared bounded into the backyard, and threw down his backpack. "Hi, Mrs. Kershner! What do you need me to do?" Jared was bouncing up and down.

"Hi boys. Thank you, Jared. You can help me put out these chairs." She waved to several chairs that were learning up against the back of the house. "These came from your Boy Scout troop and some came from church. Father Bryan brought some over."

Kevin put down his backpack and began helping.

"So have you boys talked with the other kids about their movies they're bringing tomorrow?" Mrs. Kershner asked.

Kevin and Jared looked at each other. "We saw them being made last Saturday. They look pretty good. One has a dragon and the other one apparently is about superheroes," Kevin explained.

"Wow! Then add in your movie about a three-headed alien and now we have a pretty good show tomorrow!"

Jared smiled, "Yes. It's going to be awesome!"

A truck pulled into the driveway. Sam and his dad got out.

Kevin waved. "We're back here!"

Sam came running. "Sweet!" he shouted as he looked around and gazed at the chairs. "It's our own drive-in movie theater!"

Mr. Ford, Sam's dad, came around the corner carrying

the projector. "Here it is." He patted the side of the box.

"Oh, thank you, Bill." Kevin realized he never knew Mr. Ford's first name. It was odd to hear it out loud. "You can put it on the stand there. Hopefully it will fill the screen that we put up. There is an extension cord over by the door where you can plug it in."

"I'll go get the DVD player, Mom," said Kevin.

Kevin came back out with the player, and the boys stood around anxiously waiting for the projector to be connected.

Mr. Ford made the final connections to the projector and DVD player. "Woo Hoo!" shouted Jared when the projector lit up.

Kevin took the Attack of the Three-Headed Alien DVD and popped it in.

"Wait! I want to see." Mrs. Kershner came running over.

The screen was a large white sheet that was hung from windows of Kevin's house. The light filled the home-made screen.

Kevin pressed 'play', and the DVD player whirred.

Music came from the projector and the screen was suddenly filled with the words Attack of the Three-Headed Alien.

Everyone threw their hands up in the air and cheered. The screen would work.

"We'll ask your father to connect the stereo tonight so that everyone can hear it." Mrs. Kershner patted Kevin on the back. "Thank you, Bill, for letting us borrow your projector. Well boys, it looks like we are going to have a film festival here tomorrow."

"Yes!" Jared smiled and pumped both fists in the air.

Chapter 16 Reserved Seating

The festival was going to start at 7 pm. Jared had come over at noon for lunch. He couldn't wait.

Sarah, Sam, and TJ arrived at 5:30 to help.

At 5:45 Mr. Hamner, along with Alex, and others in the movie showed up.

Mr. Hamner drove a gray SUV and everyone from their movie fit in the vehicle. He pulled up into the drive way.

"Kevin, you guys need to go out there and welcome your guests," Mr. Kershner instructed. The crew went out the front door.

"Hi, Kevin. Here is the movie." Mr. Hamner waved a DVD in the air. Mr. Hamner was tall with blonde hair parted on the side. He looked like a movie star.

Kevin's parents walked outside and introduced themselves.

"Hi, I'm Kevin's mom, Mrs. Kersnher." As Kevin's parents continued their introductions. Kevin took Alex's group around to the back where the movies would be shown.

"Movie people get their own section!" Jared grinned from ear to ear. He pointed to rows of chairs that had a paper taped with the word reserved on it.

"We have lemonade, soda, water, and of course popcorn available here in the back," Sarah waved her arm to the refreshments.

The sound of another car came from the front of the house. "Kevin, you need to come back to the front!" Kevin's dad shouted.

Kevin and the crew went back around to the driveway. Mike Jefferies, and his film cast got out of a brown mini-van. Six kids in total.

Jared waved his hand, "Hi, guys and gals!"

Mike jumped out of the van. "What's up! I see Alex is already here. Hope they didn't take the prime seats." He smiled.

"No, the casts have their own special seats," grinned Sarah. "Come on. I'll show you." She turned around and bounced down the driveway. Mike's friends followed.

Kevin went to turn around, but noticed a family coming down the driveway. "Hi, we're here for the film festival. What do we need to do?" asked the mom with three children behind her. Kevin recognized them as first graders from school.

Kevin pointed to the back yard. "Um, just follow those guys and you will see where to sit." Now that the festival was here, he was shocked that people actually showed up to see it.

"Kevin, you also need to show your guests where to get drinks and popcorn." His mom said, with her mom look on her face.

"I'll show them!" TJ raised his hand and came to Kevin's rescue and took off after the family.

"I think you, and Jared, need to stand here in front of the house to welcome people and show them where to go since this is you guys' idea in the first place," said Mr. Kershner.

"I'll go in the back and help direct people where to go Mr. Kershner," Sam said as he ran off to help in the back.

Kevin's parents stood nearby, but it was quite clear they were going to leave Kevin to do this mostly on his own.

Kevin stood in his drive and slowly more and more neighbors came walking to the house. People Kevin had known from around the street, people from school, Boy Scouts, and church were here. People he didn't know also began to arrive. People began parking on the street. More people had arrived than Kevin had ever predicted. Jared was jumping up and down beside him.

"Look at all of these people that have come to see our movies!" Just then, a tall lean African-American woman walked onto the driveway. "Hi, mom!" Jared waved.

Kevin quickly realized that he had never met Jared's mom. Jared always came over to his house. "Kevin, this is my mom."

Kevin put his hand out, "Hi, Mrs. Thompson, it's nice to meet you. I am glad you could come."

"Nice to meet you too Kevin. Jared has told me a lot about you. I am glad to know you two have become good friends."

"Is Dad coming?" asked Jared.

"He'll try. He is still at work. If he gets off in time he will come by." His mom pointed, "So, I guess I go to the back of the house?"

"Yes." Said Jared.

His mom walked to the back, and Kevin's parents stopped to talk and introduce themselves.

"Are your brothers going to come? Kevin asked.

"I don't know. I forgot to ask. I just hope my dad gets to come." Jared seemed a little sad that his dad wasn't there.

"Boys, I think the time has come to start the show!" Mr. Kershner was smiling and clapping his hands. "And I think you two need to say something to everyone here to get the show started."

Jared was ready to burst out of his skin. Kevin's stomach sank.

The time had come. The show was about to start.

Chapter 17 The Super League of Justice

Kevin and Jared walked around to the backyard. They saw all seventy-five chairs filled and some people were standing up. The yard was full.

"I guess we need to go up there and say something to get this thing started," whispered Jared to Kevin.

"You ready?" Kevin whispered back.

"You better believe it!" Jared replied.

The boys walked in front of everyone. Suddenly a cheer went up. Kevin stumbled and took a deep breath.

Sam stood up in front.

"Send in the bombers!" He yelled.

Everyone got laughed, and then settled down.

Kevin stood there rubbing his hands together. He wasn't sure what to say. He looked up and there coming around the side of the house was Mrs. Calvin, his teacher. The teacher that first encouraged him to write his daydreams in a journal. She waved. Kevin waved back.

Kevin spoke. "I want to thank everyone who came here tonight." Kevin stopped and looked at his shoes. "I hope you enjoy our Triple Creature Feature!"

The crowd cheered.

Jared patted Kevin on the back. "Yes! Thanks to everyone for being here. Let's let Alex come on down and introduce his movie." Jared pointed to Alex, and Alex came down to the front.

Alex waved. "Hi everyone."

"Hi!" The crowd responded.

"Our movie is called The Super League of Justice. I want to thank my dad for helping. And thanks to Manuel, Karen, Jeff, and Lisa for being in the movie. Anyway, I hope you enjoy it!"

Alex pointed to Mr. Ford, who was running the projector, and he began the movie.

The audience became silent. The screen went black. Suddenly music began playing and credits appeared on the screen.

The Super League of Justice in bright yellow letters stretched across the screen. The audience cheered.

A boy was running on the screen. The camera was bouncing as it followed him. He was carrying a purse. Off camera a girl was screaming, "Help! He took my purse!"

Out of nowhere an arm sticks out across the screen and the robber fell down. Alex appeared on the screen in a blue outfit with a green cowl over his face and stood over the robber.

The audience clapped and cheered.

"You know this area is under the control of the Super League of Justice! Do you know who I am?"

The robber looked up "Yes. The Blue Bug."

"Yes! I am the Blue Bug!"

Jared whispered in Kevin's ear. "That is a pretty cool costume."

"Yeah, but why does he have a green hood?" asked Kevin.

As the movie continued the Blue Beetle foiled a bank robbery, and saved a woman and her baby from a car crash. The Blue Bug went back to the Super League of Justice after his busy day and debriefed with other superheroes.

There was Electro-Woman. She was decked out in all yellow with a lightning bolt on her costume. Her hair was brushed straight back, as if she had stuck her finger in an electric socket.

"Think of the amount of hair spray that took," Jared whispered to Kevin. A couple of people shushed him for talking.

The Knight was the next superhero. He looked like a knight of the old ages, but had a force field that protected him. His uniform was updated with led lights in the elbows and knees.

"The force-field is apparently generated from those lights in his uniform," said Kevin in a hushed voice, trying not to be shushed.

While the Super League was debriefing, Alex's dad, who was playing the villain, Dr. Vespa, appeared on a video monitor that behind the superheroes.

"Why, good evening Super League of Justice," Dr. Versa growled.

"Dr. Versa! You no good rotten…" barked The Blue Bug.

"Why good evening to you Blue Bug. But enough with

the pleasantries. Right now I am holding the mayor and his daughter."

The League stood up, "Give them back!" they shouted in unison.

"Calm down. Calm down. Of course you can have them back. I have no need for them. But I will need one billion dollars in exchange." Dr. Versa smiled. "Consider it a repair cost for the last time you visited my dwelling place." He scowled.

Sarah turned around at look at Jared and Kevin. She whispered, "Mr. Hamner's pretty good!"

"Why thank you!" Mr. Hamner whispered back, from a few chairs over. Sarah blushed and turned back around to the screen.

The Super League formulated a plan, and went to find Dr. Versa and his captives. When they got to the door of his hide out, Electro-woman stuck her index finger into the keyhole and sent a surge of electricity through the door. It popped right open.

There was Dr. Versa. "Ha! Ha! You think you have me?" Dr. Versa slid down a trap down right out the room. The League followed closely behind. They landed outside in grass.

"This is the scene we saw being shot!" Jared said to Kevin.

"We were there!" Said TJ turning around. He was quickly shushed. "Sorry!" He blushed and turned around.

The scene ended with Dr. Versa being put into hand cuffs and led away. The mayor and his daughter came jumping from off screen. "Thank you for rescuing us!" exclaimed the mayor.

"The End" appeared on the screen. The crowd cheered and clapped. The cast from the movie stood up and took a bow together.

After the clapping quieted down, Kevin walked to the front to introduce the next movie.

Chapter 18 The Dragon verses the Knight

"Mike is going to introduce our next movie."

Mike came walking down the aisle and Molly followed right behind him. Mike and Molly stood to face the crowd.

"Hey everybody!" waved Mike. "I'm Mike and this is Molly. She does a great job in our movie. She's my cousin and a lot of people haven't met her so I thought I would introduce her now. So everybody, this is Molly"

"Hi, Molly!" yelled some of the students in the audience.

Molly waved back, "Hi, everyone!"

"Well, I hope you enjoy our movie!" exclaimed Alex.

"What's the name of your movie?" someone shouted from the back.

Alex smiled, "Oh, yeah! It's called The Dragon verses the Knight."

Kevin heard a few people go "Oooh!"

The movie began with Molly walking across a field in

her suit of armor. Suddenly, a group of people run across her path screaming. Off screen, a loud roar is heard and Molly looks up to see the head of the dragon. Then the title of the movie appears, The Dragon verses the Knight.

Jared leaned over to Kevin, "Smart. They didn't just open with the title." Jared nodded his head in admiration. "Smart! That's smart."

Molly pulled out her sword with her right hand and pumped it high in the air.   On her left arm she carried a shield. Molly let out a scream. She began running toward the dragon. The dragon let out a roar and flames came out of its mouth.

TJ, Sam, and Sarah all turned around with their mouths hanging wide open. "That was awesome!" Said TJ.

"We'll have to have whoever did that effect to help us on the pirate movie," said Jared. Jared was back in movie producer mode.

Molly fell down on the ground. Smoke was all around her.

"The smoke is quite clearly CGI, but still, I am impressed. Who do we need to talk to join in on our movie?" Jared wondered aloud.

A horse galloped across the screen and another knight appeared. He stuck out his hand and lifted Molly off of the ground.

"Where did they get a horse?" Jared asked with his hands in the air.

"My grandmother has a horse on her farm," said Alex from a couple of seats over.

They were shushed.

The two knights turned their horse to face the dragon. The knight that rescued Molly lifted the mask off of his helmet. "I am Sir Luke," said the knight.

Kevin knew that the knight was played by Dillon McGregor. He was a fourth grader that lived a few streets over. "Pray, what is a damsel doing dressed as a knight?" asked Sir Luke.

"I am a knight, Sir Luke. My name is Guinevere!"

"Oh, I see what they did there," said Jared.

"And if you will not help me defeat the dragon, Sir, then I shall do it myself!" Guinevere glared at Sir Luke.

"No, I will help you in your quest!" Sir Luke replied.

"We must stop the dragon! We will do best if we come up from behind and distract him from the village. We must hurry!" commanded Guinevere.

"She is quite good," said Jared.

Guinevere and Sir Luke turned their horse around, and began to gallop toward the off screen roar of the dragon.

They came upon the tail of the dragon. They climbed down off the horse, and Sir Luke jumped on the tail of the dragon. The audience laughed loudly.

The screen cut to a close-up of the dragon. He let out a stream of fire. Sir Luke and Guinevere fell to the ground as the flames shot above them.

Guinevere jumped to her feet. Sir Luke remained on the ground moaning. "I am injured, my lady! Defeat the dragon!"

Guinevere ran off screen toward the dragon. The dragon turned to face her. "Hey! This is where we came in!" said Sam to Kevin and Jared. He was immediately shushed by people near him.

A deafening roar came from the dragon and a stream

of fire. She ducked and rolled, and jumped to her feet. With one begin swing of her sword she chopped at the dragon. The screen cut to the dragon holding his side and then falling down to the ground. The dragon let out a moan and then was silent. Behind Guinevere the villagers came running carrying Sir Luke on their shoulders and cheering.

"The End" stretched across the screen and music blared.

The audience cheered and clapped wildly.

Kevin and Jared looked at each other. "That was good." They both said at the same time.

After the clapping died down, the audience turned and looked at Kevin.

It was time to introduce their movie.

Chapter 19 Start the Movie

Kevin turned and walked toward the screen. Halfway there he stopped, turned and looked the crew, and motion for them to join him at the front. "You guys need to join me up here."

Jared, Sarah, TJ, and Sam stood up and joined Kevin in the front by the screen.

Kevin looked out at his backyard and saw the scores of people in his backyard. He saw his friends from school, his parents, Mrs. Rivers, the guidance counselor, and Mrs. Calvin.

Mrs. Calvin waved and smiled. Mrs. Calvin took his tendency to daydream and turned into something positive. By recording his daydreams and fantasies he had made friends with Jared, Sarah, Sam, and TJ. He was standing here with tons of people in his backyard ready to watch a movie that he had made. He looked at Mrs. Calvin, waved back and smiled.

"Well, um, I want to thank everyone for being here. I certainly never expected this many people to come. We all want to thank everyone for coming to see Attack of the Three-Headed Alien." Kevin paused, he fumbled for words, so he gave up. "Okay, so, I guess, Mr. Ford, start the movie!"

The crowd cheered, and the crew walked away from the front.

Kevin and the crew sat down in the front row. The movie began. The opening titles in blazing yellow "Attack of the Three-Headed Alien". The audience clapped again.

The crew held their breath as the movie played. The last time they saw the movie they were sitting in Kevin's living room with just themselves as few other people.

TJ appeared as the alien on screen and the audience went quiet. TJ, sitting in the audience, grinned from ear to ear.

Sarah watching herself appear on screen blushed. Jared patted her the back.

A few minutes later Sam appeared in close-up with his army helmet and looked into the screen and yelled "Send in the Bombers!"

The crowd went wild.

The crew just sat, and soaked it all in.

The final shot appeared and the alien waved to the screen and was beamed up to his ship. The words

"The End" flashed across the screen. The crowd stood up and cheered. Alex and Mike, came up and patted Kevin, Jared, Sarah, TJ, and Sam all on the back.

"Awesome movie, you guys," said Alex.

Chapter 20 Say Movies!

After the cheering died down Kevin and the crew stood up, and were approached by just about everyone congratulating them on the movie. Kevin's dad made an announcement in a loud voice with his hands cupped around his mouth, "Thank you to everyone for coming. If you would like we have more popcorn and drinks here in the back for you to enjoy!" His dad went to the popcorn station to serve and greet people as they left.

Kevin's mom joined him at the front. "Well, it seems to have turned out pretty well," his mom said giving him a hug. "I am very proud of you! You guys did a great job with all of this!"

Mrs. Calvin made her way to the front. She gave Kevin a hug. He had never been hugged by a teacher before. "Congratulations Kevin. Your movie was great! You have a real talent for storytelling."

"Thank you for saying that, Mrs. Calvin. He has really gotten into writing since you prompted him to do it. Thank you." Mrs. Kershner smiled at Kevin's teacher.

"I am going to go so you can go be with your adoring fans. I will see you on Monday." Mrs. Calvin waved and walked away. Kevin waved back.

He was surrounded by other kids and their parents congratulating him on the movie and the festival.

Kevin just shook hands and said, "Thank you."

Kevin's dad came from the snack table carrying a camera. "Okay, I need everyone that was in a movie come stand in the front of the screen for a picture." The cast members from The Super League of Justice, The Dragon Verses the Knight, and The Attack of the Three-Headed Alien stood together with their arms around each other. "Say movies!" shouted Mr. Kershner.

"Movies!" Everyone smiled.

Chapter 21 The Clean Up

After most of the people left, the remaining parents and kids helped clean-up chairs and tables.

"Kevin it was a great idea to do this," said Sarah.

"Yes, and thank you for letting Sarah act in the movie," said a tall woman with red hair standing next to Sarah.

"Oh, this is my mom, Mrs. Rose," explained Sarah.

"Nice to meet you." Kevin shook her hand.

Mrs. Kershner came over, "Yes, thank you for letting Sarah come over. I'm Kevin's mom." They shook hands. "She's welcome to come over anytime."

"Sarah has enjoyed hanging out with Kevin and the boys," said Mrs. Rose.

"Kevin, we should begin working on the pirate movie soon," grinned Sarah.

"Oh, there's another movie coming?" asked Mrs. Rose and Mrs. Kershner at the same time.

"Yes! There is another movie coming!" said an excited Jared, who jumped in on the conversation.

"Well, let's relax from this one first," laughed Kevin's mom.

"I'll see you at school." Sarah waved and left with her mom.

"Do you need any more help?" asked Sam.

"Thank you, Sam; we've got it from here."

Mr. Ford came and shook Kevin's hand. "Kevin, nice job again!"

"Thank you for letting us borrow the projector again!" replied Kevin.

"Dudes, I'll catch you on Monday." Sam fist bumped Kevin and Jared and then left with his dad.

"Hi, Mrs. Williams." Kevin waved to TJ's mother.

"Kevin, TJ tells me you need some pirate costumes?" Asked TJ's mom.

"Not yet. Maybe later," replied Kevin.

"Thank you again, Mrs. Kershner, for hosting this. Just let me know how I can help if they want to make another movie." Mrs. Williams smiled.

"I am sure TJ will tell you when it is needed," chuckled Mrs. Kershner.

TJ fist bumped Kevin, "Catch you Monday." He left with his mom.

A tall man came around the corner.

"Dad!" shouted Jared.

"Hey buddy! Sorry I missed this." He hugged Jared. Mrs. Thompson came up and joined them.

"Hi, I'm Melanie Kershner." Kevin's mom introduced herself.

"Calvin Thompson." He shook her hand.

"I'm Gary Kershner," said Kevin's dad.

"Thank you for letting Jared hang out here a lot. I work a lot so it's nice to know he's here most of the time."

"Jared is welcome here anytime. Those two have become good friends, and Kevin has become more sociable since Jared came around." Kevin's mom said.

Kevin blushed.

"Kevin is cooler than he lets on." Jared punched Kevin in the shoulder. "I'll see you at school." Jared fist bumped Kevin, and walked away with his parents. Mr. and Mrs. Thompson waved as they left.

With no one else around, Kevin and his family went inside.

Chapter 22 And the Award Goes To…

"That was something!" Kevin's dad smiled.

"We're proud of you Kevin," said his mom. She hugged him tight. He tried to get out of the hug. He hated it when she did that.

"Mama! Stop it!" Shouted Michael, Kevin's little brother.

"Didn't we forget something?" His dad smirked. Kevin looked outside trying to see what was missed.

"I don't see anything," said Kevin.

Kevin's mom came around the corner into the kitchen carrying something gold and big.

"And the award goes to…" she smiled.

"What's this?" Kevin asked.

"It's a trophy for best screenplay and film festival!" said his dad.

Kevin took the trophy. It was a golden man holding a camera, at the bottom words were engraved, "Kevin Kershner- Best Screenplay and Producer."

"We thought about this when we showed the movie over here and you brought your friends over. It seemed to fit the evening," explained Kevin's dad.

"We are very proud of you, your stories and your friends." His mom smiled.

Kevin looked at his trophy and took it upstairs to his room.

He took out his journal.

Chapter 23 Load the Boats!

Grey Beard and Captain Kurtz stood on the edge of the Falcon. Together they knew they were close to finding The Treasure of Lima.

"Land Ho!" shouted night-watchman from the birds nest above. There over the horizon was land. Green trees and rocks could be seen in Grey Beard's spyglass.

Grey Beard leaned in and whispered in Captain Kurtz's ear. "Remember, betray me and I will run you through."

Captain Kurtz smiled at Grey Beard.

"Load the boats!" Shouted Grey Beard and the men began running to side boats ready to go to shore.

There was a knock on the door.

"Kevin get the door! It's for you!" shouted Mr. Kershner.

Kevin ran down stairs and opened the door.

There stood Jared, Sarah, Sam and TJ. TJ held up a sword and a pirate costume.

Jared explained, "We know the festival was only yesterday, but we couldn't wait."

Sarah smiled and clapped.

Jared looked back at Kevin. "Let's make a pirate movie."

The End

About the Author

Martin Tiller currently teaches fifth grade in Virginia. He lives with his wife, and daughter, and two cats, and a dog named after Star Wars characters.

Other Kevin books by Martin:
Kevin and the Seven Lions
Kevin and the Three-Headed Alien

Other books by Martin:
Dolbin School for the Extraordinary

Martin can found at martintiller.com.
You can follow him on Twitter @mctiller
You can circle him Google+
He can also be found on Amazon and Goodreads.

Carla Tracy is a UK based Designer and Illustrator, who was apparently born with a pencil in her hand, and loves nothing more than to get creative. Her first notable artistic endeavour was at Primary school, where she sculpted an entire family of Hedgehogs out of clay. She currently lives on a solitary old farm in rural Leicestershire, with her spirited little Sausage Dog as a sidekick.

Carla can found at www.carlatracy.co.uk
You can also follower her on Twitter @CarlaTracyArt

Word of mouth really helps authors and books. If you enjoyed this story please leave a review where you purchased or borrowed it. And tell a friend about Kevin!